BIG ROCK CANDY MOUNTAINS

Retold by DREW TEMPERANTE

Illustrated by STEPHANIE LABERIS

CANTATA
LEARNING

WWW.CANTATALEARNING.COM

CANTATA LEARNING

Published by Cantata Learning
1710 Roe Crest Drive
North Mankato, MN 56003
www.cantatalearning.com

Library of Congress Control Number: 2015932802
Temperante, Drew
    Big Rock Candy Mountains / retold by Drew Temperante; Illustrated by
Stephanie Laberis
    Series: Sing-along Science Songs
    Audience: Ages: 3–8; Grades: PreK–3
    Summary: Originally a traveling song about people searching for work
and adventure during the Great Depression, "Big Rock Candy Mountain" later
became a children's song about a magical place where everything is sweet and
tasty and made completely of candy!
    ISBN: 978-1-63290-374-7 (library binding/CD)
    ISBN: 978-1-63290-505-5 (paperback/CD)
    ISBN: 978-1-63290-535-2 (paperback)
    1. Stories in rhyme. 2. Mountains—fiction. 3. Candy—fiction.

Book design and art direction, Tim Palin Creative
Editorial direction, Flat Sole Studio
Music direction, Elizabeth Draper
Music arranged and produced by Steven C Music

Printed in the United States of America in North Mankato, Minnesota.
122015   0326CGS16

ACCESS THE MUSIC!

SCAN CODE WITH MOBILE APP

CANTATALEARNING.COM

Can you imagine a mountain made of sugar candy? What about a root beer **fountain** or lollipops that grow on bushes? Well, the man in this song has seen such a place.

To learn more about the Big Rock Candy Mountains, turn the page and sing along!

One evening as the sun went down
and the campfire was a-burning,
down the road came an old **hobo**.
His mind was a-churning.

I'm headed for a land that's far away,
beside the root beer fountain.

So come with me. Let's go and see
the Big Rock Candy Mountains.

In the Big Rock Candy Mountains,
there's a land that's fair and bright,
where the lollipops grow on bushes
and you sleep out every night.

Where the people all are happy
and the sun shines every day
on the birds and the bees
and the bubblegum trees.

The lemonade **springs**
where the bluebird sings,
in the Big Rock Candy Mountains.

In the Big Rock Candy Mountains,
you never change your socks.

14

And the little streams of apple juice
come a-trickling down the rocks.

The children laugh and play all day
and never go to school.
There's a lake of stew
and pudding, too.

You can paddle all around them
in a big **canoe**
in the Big Rock Candy Mountains.

In the Big Rock Candy Mountains, you'll forget all your pains.

18

And when the old folks walk around,
they lean on candy canes.

The fields, they all grow candy corn
that reaches twelve feet high
where the skies are blue
and the water, too.

Where the trees are green
and quite a scene
in the Big Rock Candy Mountains.

I'll see you all before the sugar snowfall
in the Big Rock Candy Mountains!

SONG LYRICS
Big Rock Candy Mountains

One evening as the sun went down
and the campfire was a-burning,
down the road came an old hobo.
His mind was a-churning.

I'm headed for a land that's far away,
beside the root beer fountain.

So come with me. Let's go and see
the Big Rock Candy Mountains.

In the Big Rock Candy Mountains,
there's a land that's fair and bright,
where the lollipops grow on bushes
and you sleep out every night.

Where the people all are happy
and the sun shines every day
on the birds and the bees
and the bubblegum trees.

The lemonade springs
where the bluebird sings,
in the Big Rock Candy Mountains.

In the Big Rock Candy Mountains,
you never change your socks.

And the little streams of apple juice
come a-trickling down the rocks.

The children laugh and play all day
and never go to school.
There's a lake of stew
and pudding, too.

You can paddle all around them
in a big canoe
in the Big Rock Candy Mountains.

In the Big Rock Candy Mountains,
you'll forget all your pains.

And when the old folks walk around,
they lean on candy canes.

The fields, they all grow candy corn
that reaches twelve feet high
where the skies are blue
and the water, too.

Where the trees are green
and quite a scene
in the Big Rock Candy Mountains.

I'll see you all before the sugar snowfall
in the Big Rock Candy Mountains!

Big Rock Candy Mountains

Americana
Steven C. Music

Intro

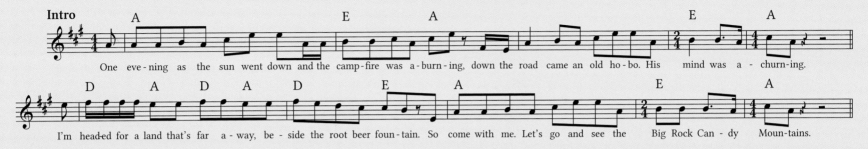

One eve-ning as the sun went down and the camp-fire was a-burn-ing, down the road came an old ho-bo. His mind was a-churn-ing.

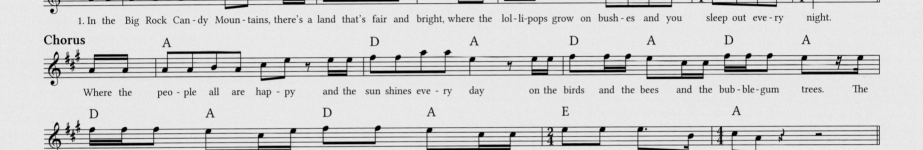

I'm head-ed for a land that's far a-way, be-side the root beer foun-tain. So come with me. Let's go and see the Big Rock Can-dy Moun-tains.

Verse

1. In the Big Rock Can-dy Moun-tains, there's a land that's fair and bright, where the lol-li-pops grow on bush-es and you sleep out eve-ry night.

Chorus

Where the peo-ple all are hap-py and the sun shines eve-ry day on the birds and the bees and the bub-ble-gum trees. The lem-on-ade springs where the blue-bird sings, in the Big Rock Can-dy Moun-tains.

Verse 2
In the Big Rock Candy Mountains,
you never change your socks.
And the little streams of apple juice
come a-trickling down the rocks.

Chorus
The children laugh and play all day
and never go to school.
There's a lake of stew and pudding, too.
You can paddle all around them in a big canoe
in the Big Rock Candy Mountains.

Verse 3
In the Big Rock Candy Mountains,
you'll forget all your pains.
And when the old folks walk around,
they lean on candy canes.

Chorus
The fields, they all grow candy corn
that reaches twelve feet high
where the skies are blue and the water, too.
Where the trees are green and quite a scene
in the Big Rock Candy Mountains.

Outro

I'll see you all be-fore the sug-ar snow-fall in the Big Rock Can-dy Moun-tains!

GLOSSARY

canoe—a narrow boat that people move through the water with paddles

fountain—a stream or spray of water used for decoration

hobo—someone who walks from place to place searching for work and adventure

springs—places where water rises from under the ground to form streams

GUIDED READING ACTIVITIES

1. In this story, there are bubblegum trees. Are bubblegum trees real? Can you name any real types of trees?

2. In the Big Rock Candy Mountains, there are many amazing things to see. What is your favorite? Why? Would you want to go to the Big Rock Candy Mountains?

3. Use your imagination and draw a land made of candy and treats.

TO LEARN MORE

Leavitt, Loralee. *Candy Experiments 2.* Kansas City: Andrew McMeels, 2014.

Rau, Dana Meachen. *Eye Candy: Crafting Cool Candy Creations.* North Mankato, MN: Capstone Press, 2013.

Tomljanovic, Tatiana. *Camping.* New York: AV2 by Weigl, 2014.

Wolf, Laurie, and Pam Abrams. *Candy, 1 to 20.* San Francisco: Chronicle Books, 2011.